anythink

For Mark
—L.S.

For my little girls—
I hope you always sing sister songs.
—T.M.-W.

Random House and the colophon are registered trademarks of Random House, Inc.

Visit us on the Web! randomhouse.com/kids

Educators and librarians, for a variety of teaching tools, visit us at randomhouse.com/teachers

Library of Congress Cataloging-in-Publication Data
Simpson, Lesley.
A song for my sister / by Lesley Simpson ; illustrated by Tatjana Mai-Wyss.
p. cm.
Summary: Mira's birthday wish comes true when her baby sister is born, but the little one spends her first eight days wailing, leaving the family at a loss for a name to announce at her simchat bat until Mira's song during the naming ceremony has an unexpected effect.
ISBN 978-1-58246-427-5 (trade) — ISBN 978-1-58246-428-2 (lib. bdg.) — ISBN 978-0-375-98004-6 (ebook)
[1. Sisters—Fiction. 2. Babies—Fiction. 3. Names, Personal—Fiction. 4. Singing—Fiction.
5. Family life—Fiction. 6. Jews—United States—Fiction.] I. Mai-Wyss, Tatjana, ill. II. Title.
PZ7.S6065 Son 2012
[E]—dc22 2011009615

MANUFACTURED IN CHINA
10 9 8 7 6 5 4 3 2 1
First Edition

A Song for My Sister

By Lesley Simpson

Illustrated by Tatjana Mai-Wyss

RANDOM HOUSE NEW YORK

I made a wish when I was three.
I shook my piggy bank over a wishing well.

Swish clink clank

The coins tumbled down.
"What did you wish?" Mom asked.
"Secret," I whispered.

My wish took four years to come true.

A sister!

Who knew someone so teeny could make
so much noise!

Waaaaaaa!

Waaaaaaaa!

"Maybe she wants
to dance," said Dad.

"Maybe she's hungry," said Mom.

Waaaaaaaa!

"Maybe that's the only sound
she knows how to make!" I said.

Waaaaaaaa!

My parents closed the windows.

"Oooh . . . cutie pie," they cooed.

"What's her name?" I asked.

"We'll announce it on her eighth day," said Dad.

"That will be her *simchat bat*—her welcome to the world."

"Do *you* have a name for her?" Mom asked.

Waaaaaaa!

"Siren," I said. "Pop her on a police car. She can wail her own name!"

"Mira!" my parents yelled. "She's your sister!"

Waaaaaaa!

I burped her.
I bounced her.
I showed her my best cartwheel.

Waaaaaaa!

I played my recorder.

I hid in my pillow fort.

Klezmer and I slept in the tree house. I put underwear in my ears.

"Her naming is tomorrow," Mom yelled over the screeching. "What are we going to call her?"

Waaaaaaa!

"What about Thunder?" I yelled back. "Did you say Wonder?" Mom shouted.

Naming day arrived.
The rabbi knocked first.

"She's fussy," said Mom.
"She's a yeller," said Dad.
"She's adorable," said the rabbi.
"Would you like earplugs?" I aske

Waaaaaaa!

Waaaaaaa!

People covered their ears. Klezmer quivered under the couch.

The rabbi began. "For sight, we hold her high so she can see the people who will love her."

Our family and friends snapped pictures, waved, and smiled.

Waaaaaaa!

"We will show her the light of a candle," said the rabbi, "so she will create light in the world."

Waaaaaaaa!

"For smell," said Mom, passing a cinnamon stick under my sister's nose.

"For taste," said Dad, tilting his *kiddush* cup. He dipped his finger into the cup.

My sister stopped crying for a minute and sucked his finger.

Waaaaaaaa!

Dad sighed. "She prefers milk."

Then it was my turn.

"For hearing, we'll sing," I said.

"Dim-dim-dee-dee-dim," I sang.

"Dim-dim-dee-dee-dim," the crowd sang back.

"Dim-dim-dee-dee-dah," I sang softly in my sister's pink ears.

She opened her eyes.

There was a hush.

"Goo-goo-ga-ga-ga," she gurgled.

"Dim-dim-dee-dee-dah," I sang.

"Duets!" The rabbi beamed. "Impressive for someone only a week old."

"Of course," I said. "She's my sister!"

My parents whispered to each other, nodding.
"Her name will be Shira," Mom announced.
"It means 'song,'" said Dad.
"Or 'melody,'" Mom added.

"Shira rhymes with Mira!" I said.

"*Dim-dim-dee-dee-dim,*" I sang.

"*Dim-dim-dee-dee-dah,*" the crowd sang back.

"*Goo-goo-ga-ga-ga,*" Shira sang again.

The next day I turned seven.
I made a wish before I blew out my candles.
"What did you wish?" asked Dad.
"Secret," I said. "A forever wish."

But I whispered into Shira's ear.
"Let's *always* sing duets. Sister songs."

Dim-dim-dee-dee-dim. Goo-goo-ga-ga-ga.